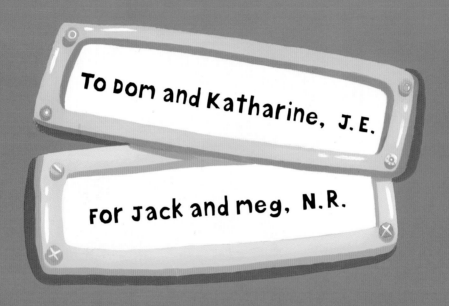

To Dom and Katharine, J.E.

For Jack and meg, N.R.

First published in hardback in Great Britain by
HarperCollins Children's Books Ltd in 2004

1 3 5 7 9 10 8 6 4 2
ISBN: 0-00-714120-3

HarperCollins Children's Books is a division of HarperCollins Publishers Ltd.

Text copyright © Jonathan Emmett 2004
Illustrations copyright © Nathan Reed 2004
The author and illustrator assert the moral right to be identified as the author and illustrator of the work.
A CIP catalogue record for this title is available from the British Library.

Visit our website at: www.harpercollinschildrensbooks.co.uk

Printed in China

You can find out more about Jonathan Emmett's books by visiting his website at:
www.scribblestreet.co.uk

What Friends Do Best

by Jonathan Emmett • illustrated by Nathan Reed

Collins

An imprint of HarperCollinsPublishers

Winston was great at building things.
He was always building something
for somebody.
He had built...

a car for himself...

...a boat for Alice

...and a motorbike for Ralph.

He had built them all by himself.
"Building things is what I do
best!" said Winston proudly.
And everyone agreed.

One morning, Ralph and Alice popped by and found Winston in his workshop looking very pleased with himself.

Passenger Weig

Ralph = 50

Alice = 0·1

Winston = 0·5

$H = \dfrac{V_{oy}^2}{2g}$

Ha
Diam
Thick

Hatch
Diameter
Thickness

Destinations (Million km)

8

0·5

1277

100 mm

200 mm

300 mm

250 mm

150 mm

$R = V_0^2 \sin 2\theta$

1

500 mm

·5mm

9

- Nozzles
- Hatches
- fins
- fixings

A

B

C

"I'm going to
build something
BIG!"
winston told them.
And he showed them
a drawing.
"That is **REALLY** big,"
said Alice. "Are you sure
you can build it all
by yourself?"
"of course!" said winston.
"Building things is
what I do best."

The next morning, three trucks arrived
and delivered hundreds of bits and pieces.
Some of the bits were very large and
difficult to carry.

"Can I help?" asked Ralph.
"I'm good at carrying
large things."
"It's all right",
said Winston.
"I can do it
myself."

But some of the bits were so large
that Winston couldn't carry them.

The next day, winston started sorting
through the smaller pieces.
some of the pieces were very tiny
and difficult to find.

"Can I help?" asked Alice.
"I'm good at finding
small things."

"It's all right," said Winston.
"I can do it myself."
But some of the pieces were so tiny
that Winston couldn't find them at all.

A week went by, and Ralph and Alice began
to get worried. They hadn't seen Winston
for days.

"He's never taken so long to build
anything before," said Ralph.
"He's never built anything
this big before," said Alice.
"Let's make sure that
he's all right."

They found Winston
sitting on the floor of his
workshop, surrounded by
all the bits and pieces.

Everything looked much the same as it had a week ago - except Winston - who looked very miserable. "Winston," said Alice, "what's the matter?"

"Everything," said Winston. "Look at all these bits and pieces. Half of them are too large to carry - and the other half are too small to find!"

"So you haven't built anything?" said Ralph.
"No!" said Winston, bursting into tears, "and building things is SUPPOSED to be what I do best."
"It's just as well we're here then", said Ralph.
"Yes", said Alice, "where can we start?"

"Don't bother," said Winston.
"I'll never build it."

"Nonsense," insisted Alice,
"all you need is a little help."
Alice sorted through the
small pieces and found the
right ones.

Ralph carried the large bits
to wherever they were needed.

And, after a while, Winston got up and started building...
which, after all, was what he did best!

They worked all day...

and all night...

And bit by bit,
piece by piece,
they put it together -
TOGETHER!

until...

...it was **done!**

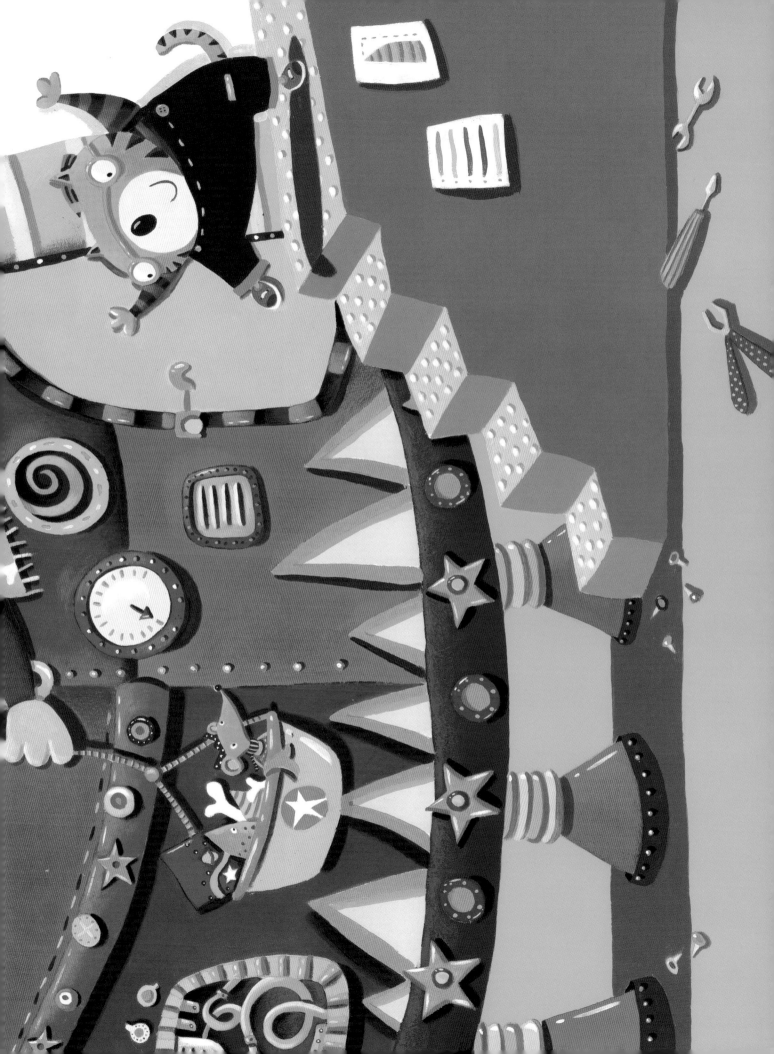

"You see, Winston?" said Ralph,
as they zoomed upwards.
"Building things really **IS** what you do best!"
"But I couldn't have done it without
your help," said Winston.

"Well", laughed Alice,
and she winked at Ralph,
"**HELPING** is what **FRIENDS** do best!"